Adelaide Climbs a Tree

By Ed Johnson
Illustrated by Caroline Devereaux

ISBN: 978-1-5356-0076-7

For my own grandparents –
wish I had known them all better.

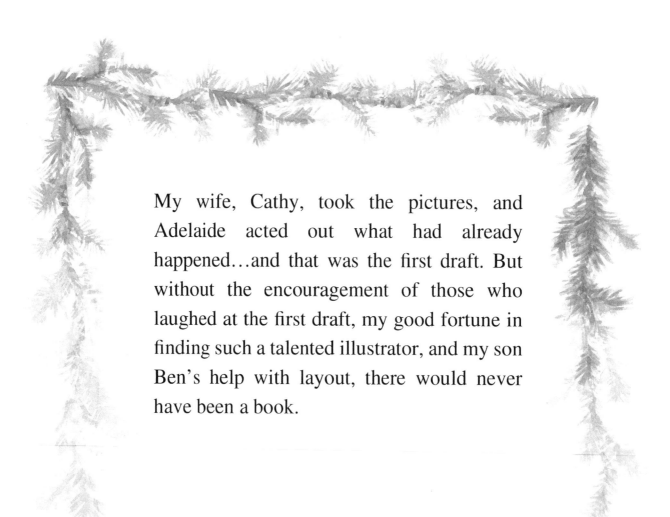

My wife, Cathy, took the pictures, and Adelaide acted out what had already happened…and that was the first draft. But without the encouragement of those who laughed at the first draft, my good fortune in finding such a talented illustrator, and my son Ben's help with layout, there would never have been a book.

My name is Adelaide
and I'm almost four years old.

This is the story of how my Grandfather
(I call him GaDa)
helped me learn how to be safe climbing trees.

The *first* time I climbed the tree,
GaDa watched from his hammock.

I climbed so high.
GaDa took a picture,
then...
I just climbed back down.

The second time
I climbed the tree,
I looked down
from the same high place.
And this time I got scared,
because I was up so high.

I hugged the tree and cried.

GaDa said,
"Are you stuck?
You climbed down
from the same place
yesterday."

I cried some more.

GaDa climbed the tree
to help me get down.
GaDa said,
"You're OK now, Adelaide."

He also said,
"This is hard on my old knees."

After we both got down safely,
GaDa and I swung in the hammock together.

He asked me if I wanted to learn how to be safe
climbing trees.

I said, "Uh-huh."

GaDa told me some rules
for safe climbing.

RULE ONE
Never climb unless
there's a grown up nearby.

RULE TWO
Never move more than
one hand...

...or one foot
at the same time.

RULE THREE
Never put your hand or foot
on a dead limb.

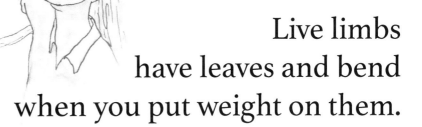

Live limbs
have leaves and bend
when you put weight on them.

Dead limbs
have no leaves
and break without any warning.

The *next* time I climbed the tree,
GaDa asked if I remembered the rules.

I said, "Make sure a grown up is nearby,
only move one hand or one foot at a time,
and never climb on dead limbs."

This time
I remembered GaDa's rules
and wasn't scared.

When I got to the same high place
I said, "I'm not stuck this time, GaDa!"

GaDa looked up
from his hammock
and said,
"Are you sure?
You look kind of stuck
to me."

I said,
"No I'm not stuck...
just watch!"

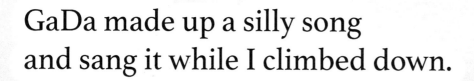

GaDa made up a silly song
and sang it while I climbed down.

"You are stuck, you are stuck,
You are really, really stuck.
You are stuck, off the ground,
You are stuck, and you can't get down.
Ha ha ha, you are stuck.
Ha ha ha, you are stuck."

When I got to the bottom, GaDa said,
"What's this?
I thought you were stuck,"
and we both laughed.

GaDa likes to joke with me
because he likes to hear me laugh.

CPSIA information can be obtained at www.ICGtesting.com
Printed in the USA
BVIW12n0244290816
460474BV00022B/246